**Other Books by Allen Frost**

*Ohio Trio: Fictions* (Bottom Dog Press 2001)

*Bowl of Water* (Bottom Dog Press 2003)

*Another Life* (Bird Dog Publishing 2007)

BIRD DOG

PUBLISHING

# Home Recordings

## Allen Frost

**Harmony Series**
**Bird Dog Publishing**
**Huron, OH**

Bird Dog Publishing
PO Box 425
Huron, OH 44839
An Imprint of Bottom Dog Press, Inc.
http://smithdocs.net
Bird Dog Publishing Homepage:
http://smithdocs.net/BirdDogy/BirdDogPage.html

Credits:
Cover Photo by Allen Frost
All drawings by Allen Frost
Author Photo by Rosa Frost
Layout and Design by Larry Smith

The poem "Uncle Charley" first appeared in
*Come Together: Imagine Peace* (Bottom Dog Press 2008)

# Contents

## While the Rest of the World

She can tell our story
with art and words
while the rest of the world
is in the dark

Let her tell you
what she sees
open up to her view
she can reveal
she knows what's real

While others say nothing
she has a light
and the talent to live on
down through the ages

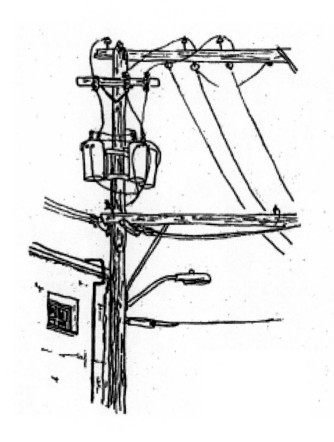

## Filming Caruso

The idea arrived in the phantom light of 2 AM.
A 50 watt bulb on a cord clicked on, notes were
hurried down until they were done.

In the morning I was at the café washing dishes.
Think about the storyline while the machine keeps
rolling out white plates and steam.

Long after a forty cent meal from a box,
I sat with a cup of coffee and explained to Mike,
"The film is called Caruso." I stopped to let it
sink in to another sip of coffee. Just the name
should roll upon the air like thunder.
While I waited for my Director's reply,
the waitress came by and I caught her arm,
"More coffee please."
She paused and dead-pan delivered,
"Would you like to order any *food* with that?"
"No," I told her. "Coffee's fine."
She was slow about it though. While she poured
by drop, I laid out the story-line across the table.
"Here it is," I said. "Read it and weep."

We saw our camera waiting for auction,
numbered on a shelf with Bermuda souvenirs
and radio-controlled toys. First we had to wait
through the antics of fishing poles being sold
by the cowboy calling from his cage above.
"What about this stereo?" his voice rodeoed
"Jim, turn that on, let the folks hear it."
A shriek of noise wouldn't stop.
"Jim, turn that off!"
We watched poor Jim struggle with the bent dials
He mumbled something up. The cowboy yelled
on and on at him. The crowd sat in folding chairs,
fanned the heat with folded magazines. At last,
Jim followed orders and unplugged the set.
The charge died. Some neon signs were next to go

before the cowboy finally ordered Jim to hold out
the Super-8.
"Seven dollars!" I heard the Director shout.
Miraculously, that was enough. Everyone else was
waiting for junk.

Black and white Super-8 film is a thing of
the past. As of that day, we had bought the last of it.
Whatever was left would have to be enough.
Filming began on a sunny day in the graveyard.
We parked the borrowed car next to a slate colored wall
and got out. Make-up was applied to my feet (cornstarch
and water, dots of red ink) and I fitted the pig mask over
my head.
It needed a retake to film the simple path of pig
between cemetery stones; the Director was laughing
and the camera shook like a candle landslide.

Painted on the wall was the Budget descent,
figured in pennies. The minute we lost to laughter
had cost us six hundred of them.

The next bright day was all railroad shots.
Pitiful feet dragging shoes on the tracks. Some
Mexicans pulled up chairs beside the blackberries
to be entertained. The heat of the sun in the mask
was unbearable.

At the mortuary, I was chased down
the steps by a pale ghoul in a dark suit. At the
traffic roundabout, the Director risked his life
leaning out of a circling car, camera rolling at 40
miles per hour. A Russian tourist slurred advice.
A pigeon shadowed over the bricks in Chinatown
where the missions were early dawn releasing the
bleary back to the streets. A church service was
interrupted to capture their slamming door on film.
I couldn't afford a nail for a prop, so I stole one from
the hardware store. And more seconds and minutes
were taken from the air.

For a moment we considered giving
the reels to a someone somebody knew.
There was a bathtub involved. Picture it
with lion claws, a rusty ring, filled deep
with chemicals and the seaweed kinks of our
developing film.

In the end, we chose to run the Budget
into the ground. Check enclosed, Caruso was mailed
off in a yellow envelope with the imposing return
address: MGM Jr. A couple of weeks would
have to pass.

The news arrived fast as I pulled the last load
of glass from the dishwashing machine. The Director
clawed at the screen door like a firefly. "It's here!"
he gleamed. Yesterday we had rented the editing
equipment by posing as college students, tonight
we could hammer out the film seam by seam.

A little crank pulled the film through.
Peering over his shoulder, I watched the smallest
window reveal white leader, then black.
Slowly, as if driven by Bela Lugosi in a
cape, the black ebbed away, leaving the title
shimmering . . . Caruso.

Fevered, we strung the midnight basement
room with clotheslines. Bit by bit, we cut lengths
of celluloid and numbered them with tape.
The story hung from spider webs.
Sticking them all together into one roll
took the moon a long journey towards Japan.
By the phantom light again, we watched in awe:
the fade into trees, cut to a rose in a garden, written
The End.

## Hubert Faucet

Hubert Faucet, champion dreamer of the world
walks on his own stares on a carpet unrolled
wearing a vaudeville show

In the spring, birds fly a crown
he will set up court on your lawn
hush the city
turn off every out-of-tune sound
ask that all traffic stop, cars and buildings bow
the ground is felt and flowers taught to grow

## Bob Hope

One night, he called the operator, forgetting it was late.
Of all the people in America, sleeping or somewhere
involved in the dawn, he wanted to talk to Bob Hope.
"I don't know his number, I'm not sure where he is,"
he said. "He might be in Hollywood, or maybe it's
Miami Beach." The operator paused not so pleasantly.
She hated this part of her job, she was just waiting
for her next coffee break. "I'm sorry sir, but I'll need
a destination. There are names in every city in
every state that are the same." He listened and
sadly sighed. Millions of Bob Hopes, lost in crowds
of any town, cast like Halloween masks afloat.

## Migrating Birds

Over the rained on field
littered with pumpkins
broken shards like pottery

## For Themselves and the New World

The last music played inside the barn
by a rockabilly trio from Tennessee
They traveled in a dented car in the 1950s
stopping in all the towns with a scene
playing loud drums and guitars making a name
for themselves and the new world following.
They were on television and sang on radio,
it became popular to know who they were.
That was forty years ago and now
they're like the barn
leaning in the wind.

## Music Is Everywhere

Turn down your radio
it's time to go
up on the roof
and listen to
the wind blown night

## The Instrumonster

Her bedroom had a little door
that opened to the attic. In the daytime
the red wallpaper danced on it, but at night
it was very dark. When she lay in bed with
the covers over tight, she would just wait
for the music to start.
A creak was its violin. Then the distant
sound that could be a train, she knew was
really a trumpet muffled by fur. Playing
its part, a cello might start to whisper
right over the chair. And the monster
must be fast, for she swore she could hear
a drum rapping softly by the window.
If all of the instruments played at once
everyone in the house would know.
The monster was smart, the band
played along, one by one
until the song would spell
her to sleep.

## The Bazooka Joe Mystery

It was supposed to be a mystery
rivaling the adventures of Sherlock Holmes
or at least worthy of the Boxcar Children.

Our daughter has been having trouble sleeping
every night her call wakes us to go downstairs
to her room. It's true, it can be noisy sometimes
outside her window at night, with people
walking on gravel, cars and headlights.

Looking for the end of insomnia,
we took the bunk apart and brought
her bed upstairs around the stairway.
Maybe she feels too apart from us.

I even started hiding Bazooka Joe gum
under her new pillow. I was hoping
to delight her and make her wonder
if the Tooth Fairy was around.

But that part of the night
was easy for her to figure out
she knew right away it was me.

## The Second Time

They decided to wait until winter to cut at the blackberry bushes piled behind their house. When January set in across everything, the vines would shed their leaves and snake back to burrow, then they could cut them and rake the ground and turn it into a garden in Spring. It would be good to have it gone. In August they picked ripe berries to make their last ever jam and pies.

Early in December, snow fell, but they were going to wait a little longer. The vines tangled in the cold.

Wearing double layers of clothes, Elmer Ford marched up and down the hall, ringing a bell. This was the morning they had all been waiting for. Children came running through doors. Outside, they fell around the frozen vines and sliced at them with rakes and wooden swords. Elmer even tied a rope from the bumper of his Model T and dragged roots out of the ground. That's how he dislodged the tube. It was plowed out of the earth like a bomb, it sparkled as something golden from Mars in the weak sunlight.

Elmer's children were making drum noises on it with their rakes and weapons when he got out of the tin car and made them stop. He examined the steel hollow tube and he found letters on it, underneath the dirt and weeds. Already one of his sons had discovered a silver door handle on the side and he turned it open. The hiss of steam threw them all backwards, they stared as a tall man stood up.

It was him, it was Abraham Lincoln. He put on his stovepipe hat to shade his eyes from the glare of the twentieth century America. To get his bearings here, in a ruin of blackberry vines fifty years after the war, he cleared his throat and gave the Gettysburg Address again.

## The Set To Pop Parking Lot

There I was, no training at all in delivering
babies, working with a teenager who was nine
months pregnant. Every morning she was closer.
"I'm set to pop," she kept telling me. It made me
a little worried. "Look..." I finally said. A cold wind
from the lake blew between all the cars we walked
around, inspecting them for stickers. "I'd really
appreciate it if you didn't pop when I'm around."
I was exhausted with the worry, it was actually
keeping me up at night. I even had a book from
the library, but I couldn't get past the first chapter.
I told her honestly, from the heart, "There's just
no certainty I'd be able to help you. Don't expect
any heroics. I know I'm being heartless, but if
you pop, I'm sorry, there's no guarantee."
She laughed at me and pulled her shirt over her
round swollen belly. A red balloon floated up,
tied by a string to her navel. She held it softly
between her hands and she showed me.
Inside, moving, suspended in the fluid,
a little child lived. "This is my baby," she
smiled, all aglow. "And when I'm ready,"
she held a pin next to the balloon, "I will
pop."

## The Smallest Cigarette Wind-Up Toy

In Central Park today, escaping from the office for
the green wind of statues and pigeons, I was eating
a cheese sandwich under the singing trees.
I heard a girl cry for help. Already the voice
seemed further away, leaving on a miniature train,
so I almost tripped over her in my running to
discover. When I found her, she was the height
of a coke bottle. She was fast shrinking away,
yelling out and waving her arms towards me.
It was the smallest cry for help I've ever heard.
But there was nothing I could do (thinking
maybe I should cup my hands around her
like a carbonated matchstick) but I could only
watch her shrink into a Camel box shadow
and blow away like the smallest cigarette
wind-up toy.

## The Witch of East Maple

Unfortunately, she didn't get very far
on the last sunny day of winter.

Her broom swooped down the incline
from her shuttered house on the hill,
veered into the car wash bay.

Caught in hot water evaporation
only the weight of her stick
made it through to the other end.
The broom hit the pavement
like a dead branch.

## Teen King

The sound of Eddie Cochran can just faintly be heard through the pour of water. Then a hand over the hood of the Toyota and Teen King appears, white t-shirt and blue jeans, pompadour and an unlit cigarette stuck to his curling sneer. "This one's done!" he slapped the shiny waxed surface with a rag and inside of it Jerry popped the clutch and sped it out into the parking lot. T.K watched it go, laughed and turned around for the next car in line, a Mercedes convertible.

At night, he set his tape deck on repeat so the Elvis Presley Sun Sessions played over and over again. And that voice that he knew and felt in him just like blood would sing to entrance the rattling windows and heavy click of freight car wheels outside, while Teen King fell asleep and dreamed of the better America.

He wondered things, as he walked over the bridge connecting him back to the land where the carwash was in the middle of town. He tossed pennies from way up in the air and watched their copper spin twinkle into the dark mud below. Teen King wasn't like the rest, he kept good music in his head, when he went places he thought of crackling vinyl melodies.

Friday night, he and his girl went to the pictures, a double feature of *East of Eden* and *In A Lonely Place*. Then they stopped for coffee at a café. It was alright, she had a piece of chocolate pie too and she smiled when he broke his cool angle posture long enough to lean over and kiss her. She talked about school and shared a cigarette and glowed when some friends showed up to see her with the guy who dropped out. Teen King didn't like the music they played for fifty cents a song on the new juke box, he mumbled something about how when the music was wrong then the entire country was wrong.

Finally, he reached over the table and pulled her hand and they went out to where the night was blue, but light enough to see the moon silver on the railroad tracks making a path back to his room. She put on her favorite Platters record so the neighbors couldn't hear them through all the cheap wooden walls as they unbuttoned each other to lay down.

Sometime during the night, he decided it was now or never. She was warm and jigsaw puzzled around him and he woke her up out of her gentle sleeping when he sat up on the edge of the bed. It sounded like a drunken fight maybe two floors above. She rolled and held out an arm, "Come back..." Teen King promised he'd be right back, he pulled on his clothes, he felt restless, there was something he needed to do. The bed swayed while he bent over to put on his shoes. She got dressed too, stood with him beside the door, followed beside as they both went to the street and disappeared along the moon's thread of light.

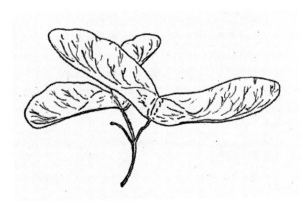

## Finding Calm in a World War

It was a place he would go every morning, the ocean was just across the reeds and dunes and his house was off through the pine woods about a mile from here. There was a small pool of water before him, birds hopped on the branches and cattails, it was a calm place to think, he felt a presence radiating from it. No one else knew about it, he followed the winding deer paths in tall grass to get there. It was quiet.

After a while, he would stand up and return to his parked car. Back among people, the gas stations and fast food restaurants and real estate offices of the town. He always wondered what it was like before everything became America. Once he drove to the Indian reservation, but whatever it used to be seemed to be lost. There were only these very small places left.

Two hundred years ago, he thought, watching the minnows making circles on the pond. There wouldn't have been all the money worries, he wouldn't have been evicted from his house. He was being forced to the city, to get a job there. The only times he had gone to Seattle, he had been overwhelmed by the noise, the crazy traffic, telephone poles and tall buildings bending all overhead.

He sighed and breathed in the air and feeling of this place. It might not even be here when he returned from Seattle with money to pay bills. There were bulldozers a half mile away. He wished there was some way to protect this place, but all the land around here was being bought and sold and rolled over.

He thought of the stillness that seemed to glow from this place, he imagined it encircling him like a bubble and he let it have magical power. He concentrated on the invisible curve, making it strong enough to be a shield. Machinery would crash up against it, America would rage and bang all around it, but could never get inside. Satisfied, he opened his eyes and stared.

Surfaced in the pool of water, rusted, laid over with green weeds, an old Japanese mine waited just long enough for him to recognize it, then it sank back below.

## Becoming

She was feeling like the moss and chamomile weeds
that grow from the sidewalks. Wherever she blew,
she kept her eyes low and down under the looks of
people going around her. She went through the hissing
doors of Safeway, lurked past the cashiers and buyers
in lines and she joined the wake of a shopping cart
down Aisle 5. The tall woman in front of her stopped
at the rice and picked through the plastic wrappers.
The girl behind her slowed and froze
becoming a shadow of the woman,
staring at herself mirrored, only years older.
She wanted to speak but she was scared—
what do you say when you meet yourself?
Was there anything she should know—
things to avoid or places to go?
Then the woman noticed her there, smiled
same eyes lit up like forever burning stars.

## The Laurel & Hardy Liberation Army

Posie Crutchfield, very old on a black creaking
bicycle, turned down an alley and rattled
cobblestones. She rode onto a two by four
slanting up onto scaffolding framing a brick
building. Like a sparrow hopping branches
in a bare winter tree, she went up and up
to the very top. She stopped. A hundred feet
from the ground, she pushed the bike up on
its kickstand so the back wheel was free to
spin. She opened the box latched on handlebars,
a gleaming silver and green projector revealed.
She fed a reel of black film into the spool and
set the switch, pulled a string, then pedaled
the movie into rolling. A little yellow candle
lightbulb was glowing. Across the drop,
images and slogans magically appeared
on the opposite wall. Above the roofs
and traffic, the cold city, tired and dark
and gray from long winter days, was given
a chance to see Laurel and Hardy comedies.

# The Cold White Sock

When they went to school that morning,
three boys puffing steam in the cold air
there it was in the blades of grass
a cold white sock
Ice seemed to grow from it
and immediately one boy
dared his friend to put it on

The jeers began to saw
until the boy gave in
took off his boot and sock
and put the thing on

He took it off right away
but there was a cold
that never left that day

When he got home and sat
in the kitchen and told his mother
she heaved the kettle full of hot
silver water and made him
put that little foot in

## Henry Snowed

Stranded in town during a blizzard
so bad the buses couldn't run
we stood in the snow
up to our knees
and watched the city sink.

Luckily, Henry knew someone
a girl who lived above the Ave
and she let us stay on her floor
so there we were overnight.

In the morning light
we had some breakfast there
while an old man sat in a chair
in the corner with his book,
blaring the radio reports.

We left, crunched through
the snow on our long walk
back to our rented house.

Henry took out the sugar cube
a perfect white little square
she had given him to share.
Broken in half on his palm
it didn't take long before
we felt the change.

## Ufology

They made some mistakes in the past.
In the 1950s they used to fly over deserts
near highways or flash by in the night sky
where small towns grew. That's how they made
their presence first known. Shooting through
the air in their silver glowing spaceships,
disappearing at the blinking speed
of light, but people took them
the wrong way.

Films were made about them
landing and taking over with
superior technology and weapons,
frightening powers unheard of.
Since then, they've decided to
become more careful on this world.
They seldom use their flying saucers
leaving them covered by tarps
in garages. Now they prefer
to travel by car, it's easier that way.
In blue Pontiacs they coast along
the highways at midnight
driving beneath the stars.

## Everything Began Across the Sea

I always think of your English eyes
it's a long time I've walked up stairs
paced by the brick fireplace
chosen words so carefully
you must go to sleep to meet me.

Everything began across the sea
Hampstead Heath and Rolling Green,
the raining top and moving spirit
hills slouching on the way to London.

Silver and stone gray memory
learn from the passing of trains
checkerboard pattern of fields
glowing going back to where
it all started with your breath.

## Until I Woke in Surprise

I tried all night to listen
to the rain on the rooftop
like a Japanese painting
the quiet water sound
seemed to never slow

It wouldn't stop
until I fell asleep

Then dreams appeared
black and white movies
I was living in another world
until I woke in surprise and knew

# Henry's Shadow

She had a rented room at the top of the stairs
a stone's throw or so from the highway

Memory has transformed it into a castle tower
walled with dark tapestries and candle electricity

Henry and I took the bus from work in that mad rush,
he wanted me along, I was the shadow
who followed him there

So I stood by the window downstairs
and listened for a while, caught between
the murmur of cars and them upstairs

I guess I decided after a while I better go
creaked on the stairs to let them know
and stopped at her open door

They sat on the floor
everything they had said
lay broken all around them
all the time they had spent,
long-stemmed memories
lay shattered in pieces of statue
or petals torn and thrown down

I could see it plainly
that's the way it goes
I thought I should be leaving
but Henry had to go too

They were both done
it was so quiet in the room
even the traffic had died
like blood gone cold

## Next to an Ocean

Fishing now
for broken hearts
where loneliness
most hurts

When dawn arrives
swept up in tide
they catch
on silver hooks


## What Happened in Seattle

The ghosts that arrive in
big ancient looking sailing
ships disguised as clouds
take over town with their
influence of gloom and
inspiration like what
happened in Seattle

## Pollution

I have taken that knotted
feeling out of my chest
and unrolled it out over
these bricks at my feet

It could have been a dark kite
or a pirate sail pulling me along
now it's nothing, thin as rice paper
torn by the shoes that I wear

## The Paper Trash

The paper trash
decorates the creek
folded into origami
by the passing trees

## Dream Machinery

There's no reason to sink
any further underneath

We had our inventions
the aeroplane
motorcar, highways
the Empire State Building

We controlled electricity
technology, industry

We saw the universe
from telescopes on mountains
everyday we were getting closer

As long as I can remember
we desperately reached out
at the furthest thing away

Just like any broken part
of that dream machinery
let it go if
it doesn't seem to work
trade it in for something
that will

## Henry vs. Waldo

Waldo was the one
who took it upon himself
to go raid the construction site
at night to get the boards
they didn't use during the day

The heat had been
cut off and of course
it had to be the coldest
winter on record in years
so we had to make do
with what we could find

Waldo brought home
2x4s and like some
maniac with strength
he would snap them
into pieces on the path
in front of the door

Try breaking a 2x4
slamming it down
Henry did and
the shudder made him
have to sit down and
grip his knees

Waldo knew the weak point
somehow exactly where
each piece would split
when hit on that spot

None of us could figure it out
we could only watch Waldo's
caveman display and be
happy once those boards
made it into the fireplace

On the mantelpiece above
stood Waldo's sacred books
written down by his guru
and who were we to ask why,
but one night drinking wine
brought home from work
Henry did

He and Waldo were gone
into conversation
the candles burnt low
Suddenly Henry pushed it
"Okay," he said
"If material things mean
nothing to you, then
what about these?"

And he was on his feet
the fireplace was burning
with 2x4s and the green
light from half the couch
sawed and thrown in too

From the jagged
last parts of the couch
I watched Henry sweep
Waldo's books off
into the fire

Oh, there followed
a moment where I thought
everything would burst

It got so quiet
as the paper burned
and died down

Waldo did too—
after all, he knew
the loss of anything

written down
was already
in his heart


## The Hitler Cat

I don't think I've mentioned
the Hitler Cat before
I can't remember exactly
where I used to see him
as he emerged from low ivy
on a well worn pathway

I laughed when I recognized
the moustache and slicked
black hair across his white face
the absolutely terrified look
he gave me back

It's been 50 years
reincarnation from
the lowest life forms
starting all over again

Actually it's a lesson
appropriate to our time
to witness that cat
who runs along cement
in fear and memory

## Curtains

I'm glad
I can go

I know
someday
I have to


## Haunting

One of those places with a sign
drilled on the lawn For Rent
the house an empty echo
we clomped in late at night
flipped open black cases
a trumpet and a clarinet
walked in the dark warming up
room to room, slow and around
haunting with Mood Indigo

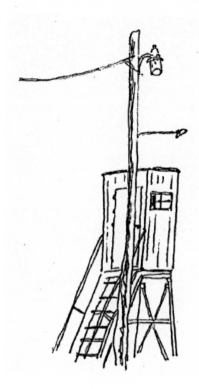

## Mike's Birdhouse

We would ride to where
the concrete of the city
broke off into the bramble
banks of the Columbia
park our bicycles
under the freeway

The highway roared
pyloned up overhead
factories and warehouses
beside the dumpster

We had to climb its side
and pry open the door
to get inside and
what a sight
to behold

As daylight fell in
we echoed all over
the pine cut scraps
stacking our hands full
it was a sort of paradise
at a time when I used to
make toys and boxes
and giraffes five feet tall

I built a nest in the basket
of my black English one-speed
Mike filled his backpack
then we rode Hawthorn home

As if filmed by time lapse
over the next few hours
we made birdhouses

They were strange looking
we made them that way
mine never left the bookshelf
Mike took a porcupine vision
spiny with nails
up into the eaves

It didn't seem possible
that pointed contraption
would collect any birds
the air was too big
the city was so wide

When they did arrive
like watching a cartoon
in a little wooden television
a pair of sparrows
found Mike's birdhouse
stuffing it with weeds
to cushion the nails
and the Spring filled it
with bird sounds

## The Coney Island Carpet Pet

Coney Island's tall metal carrousel flower rusts up tall over the sand and overlooks a fenced off lot where its shadow sounds as small as pollen along the chain link. There's an opening in the fence, the wire is bent and pulled aside like a circus tent flap, two feet, enough to pass through on hands and knees. Scattered on the ground, cans, bottles, stones, broken machinery metal dead like industrial wildflowers. Crashed dirigibles of nails, bolts and strips of orange steel. Old clown paintings with strange teeth glare from plywood walls. Looking down over the fence, the Octopus ride has curled up with its arms closed in the shadow of a tall gray falling down building. All the space of dirt and pavement is littered so walking is really careful navigating. Every step is cold winter on the fairgrounds. In the center of the lot lies a stack of mattresses, carpets and tarps discarded, thrown like an unlucky pile of cards. There is a caved opening close to the earth leading into the dark underneath. For only a second as I look inside, a dog appears in the light. A brown dog with a white stripe on its face, a wild animal, crouching, staring then vanishing to the quietest voice calling it back into the black of Coney Island under carpets.

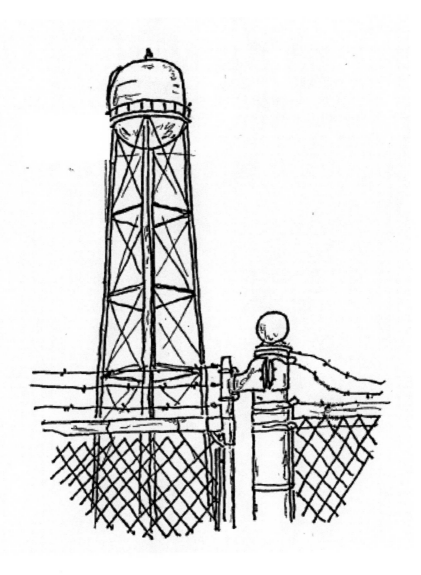

## How My Great-Grandparents
## Met in Scotland

He went back to the homeland, sailed recrossing
the ocean to look for her. The early 20<sup>th</sup> century
streets, the cobblestones and sun. She was with
a friend, walking, they had just come from a
gypsy fortune teller. She was told of a dark
stranger arriving from a faraway place and
her heart was set on waiting for him to find her.
He met her on the street that day and he could
see in her all the love that couldn't be found
in America.

# The Three Candles

The Seattle Wax Museum is gone now, I'm not sure
where it disappeared. Apartments have been built
over its site and those stacked rooms are probably
being haunted by wax visions of Abe Lincoln,
John F. Kennedy, the pioneer founders of Seattle,
Neil Armstrong, Lindbergh, Marilyn Monroe,
The Beatles and a cast of characters I've since
forgotten. I do remember there used to be
the Three Stooges, as real as they were on TV
but in three dimensions, roped off from us...
I wonder if they were auctioned off when
the wax museum went under? Maybe it
was a bargain, someone bought them for
only $120. The statues came with simple
temperature instructions: keep out of
direct sunlight and away from any heat
source. "Naturally!" the person who
bought them laughed, "They're wax!
They'll melt!" So he cloaked them over
in bedsheets and drove them away,
onto Interstate 5, going South.
When he got to Spirit Lake,
he found the airport and chartered
a helicopter. It let him off on the summit
of Mount Saint Helens. There, he arranged
the three infamous wax players in the ice
and set up his expensive camera equipment.
A panorama of breathtaking blue and
white, at the top of the world with
Larry, Moe and Curly. It could have been
one of their films from long ago, as he bent
his finger to record the scene. But history
had other plans. The ground began to shake,
knocking everything down as the volcano
exploded with hot ash. It was probably
the tremor or was it a some other force
that carried across the miles from there,
suddenly waking me from a dream.

## Blues With a Mummy

Hopping trains, hitchhiking and taking rides with cross country truck drivers whenever they could, the two musicians traveled the weary south with their guitars and their mummy King Ibis. He was light as paper, they carried him in a long cardboard painted box, with handles like a suitcase. Whenever they stopped to play the blues, on some Mississippi street corner or decayed wooden Georgia dancehall, they'd open the coffin for people to see King Ibis, draped with a red satin sheet, frozen inside.

Nobody really knew where he came from, maybe he really was a Libyan pharaoh like the two men claimed in the act. People watched in quiet, almost scared of what he might do with the sad music. They always managed to barely survive, America was a big place, they could move on the roads all their lives and never see the same places twice. They kept hoping for better things.

In New Orleans, they nearly lost King Ibis in a heated poker game. Once, they threw him out of a hotel window to dodge the police. A flood nearly took him out to sea. Bullets like bees chased them out of a speakeasy. Wherever they went, he was along for the ride.

Then in Tennessee, on a flatbed car late at night, he was struck by lightning. Miraculously, it gave him life again. From then on he flew out of the coffin when they played and he danced to the music furiously.

It was no small change anymore, crowds paid when they passed through. People needed them. Like genie gold, King Ibis transformed their act and while he creaked and flew in circles with dust, they sang loudly together on the spotlit stage, discovered at last.

## The Dummy Family

We created an entire family for only a few dollars
clothes, hats and shoes all bought at Goodwill
stuffed with newspapers, then placed in lying-down
tragedy on the pavement of Maine Street at night.
They looked real enough to stop traffic and
brought on the police with blue lights.
We dragged the dummies home in a panic,
over fences, across lawns in the dead of night
We flopped them down on our apartment floor
and left them there. The Dummy Family was
a terrible failure. Still, they survived.
They spent a week thrown underfoot
like dead shadows beneath a pier.
Then one afternoon, I had a plan.
The father's fall was just my size.
I took out his newspaper stuffing
and climbed into his Goodwill clothes.
I lay in his place on the floor and waited.
It was a terrible wait, I couldn't move,
I couldn't laugh and give it away as the door
handle finally rattled. A friend came inside
and sat by a guitar. He started to play.
I watched through a little tear in newspaper
until I couldn't take it any more. I leaped up
shouted, waved my arms at someone
I had shocked into seeing a ghost.

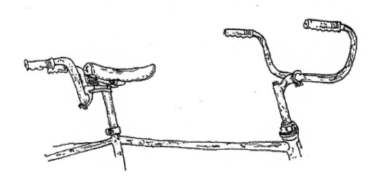

## Visiting Arnold

Visiting Arnold is what he called it. Every few days
or so, he would reach that point, he would have to
saddle himself to that old bicycle left in the weeds
at the side of the house. Two miles down the street
he would hook onto Holly and glide downtown.
No pedaling at all, he would ride on the downhill
edge of car traffic, magic carpeting over land,
stopping at the gotham feet of the Carroll
Apartments. The building soared from the ground
like a church organ, tiered up to where birds made
specks at the top. Going in the doors, he was
transformed. In the lobby, if he happened to see
someone he knew, they would hail him,
"Hello Arnold!" He would wave back, smile
and small talk. Then Arnold would take the elevator
to his floor. The smell of the old carpets, the faded
wallpaper swirls, he was far from the dream version
of the man who kept that golden key on a hook
in a garage.

## Hamburger Song

For an hour
he watched
the singing star
from Georgia
across a table
in a chair
with a notebook
and a coffee

He got
close enough
to read
his labor
one word
all it said:
Hamburger

## The Deli 5

Over the course of seasons, with my chair pushed in the corner and an eye on the stage, I observed the change. The first time I recall them at the deli was in the winter. I'd been going there on and off when the mood struck me, it had been a sort of harbor for me to come in out of the wind.

Also, I had developed a sweet tooth for that carrot cake they make. A slice of that and a black coffee served in a ceramic cup, and I was quite content. So it was, when I looked up from my corner to see the five of them.

The deli fills up the ground floor of an old yellow house in my neighborhood. Though the space had been remodeled to accommodate tables and chairs, walls have windows to other rooms, it's still like being at home, with a lamp beside me and a plant trailing down. But calm enough to feel the balance tip when they walked in with their standup bass, French horn, guitar, drum and accordion. They captured my attention even before they started to play. I stared, I couldn't help it, through the doorway arch to where they set up against the wall near the silver and glass counter display.

That first day they didn't get very far, a couple songs. Each time someone tried to get past the big bass to order, the instrument had to bend aside, and the melody would lose its way. Finally it was gone for good—the wooden hips of it tipped and swiveled and were walked right out. That was that.

The four members of what was The Deli 5 showed up again a couple weeks later. I knew they were returning when I saw their sign, The Deli 4. I made sure I was there, I had my usual seat, my usual meal, and I was waiting.

What came in was an argument. The French horn player didn't even make it in, with the door held open to the rain and slick sounds of tires driving by. I held my coffee and listened, as did everyone, to the end of The Deli 4.

"Fine! It's The Deli 3! I like that better anyway!"

The three who stood draining in the old living room stayed there a little more but they didn't play that day.

Everytime I walked by the Yellow Deli, I looked for their sign in the window. Something must have happened though. It got warmer, rained the cold away and green leaves and flowers began lives.

One day, I spotted a torn violet handbill stapled to a telephone pole. The Deli 2, it claimed. They were playing, but the paper was ripped, I couldn't tell where. Why does it matter, why should I care? My appetite for carrot cake had waned too, I wasn't in the mood. Things change.

It was deep in spring when a sunny noontime brought me back with the thought of glazed pear, the faintest taste of cinnamon. I even hoped for music again.

I don't know what kept my interest in The Deli 5, just one of those small story things I suppose, like waiting for some rare species of butterfly or bird to return. Of course any time I was at the deli, I would think of them, until that spark turned into my served food, then the comfort of that joined the pages I was reading.

I was halfway through my pie and *Madame Bovary* when music began in the other room. I don't think the city had a person so happy as me to hear that heartbroken accordion wheeze into life songs of betrayal and sorrow, the bleak poetry of human existence and weight of the world heaped on The Deli 1.

## Rabbit String

When the rabbit
leaves in the grass
only one tall stalk
is left trembling
a string of music
this morning
only I can hear

## All Shakespeare's Birds

Edward Shepherd stepped out of the elevator carrying a suitcase filled with birds. After the cold winter air of Lima, Ohio, the sudden warmth of the red planet hit him like a wave. He wore his best tan searsucker suit, he swung the suitcase lightly as he stepped onto Mars.

This was his second trip to Mars. The first time, half a year ago, he'd been struck by the bare violet sky, awfully empty. He took it upon himself to change that. When he went back to America, he grabbed every bird he could, collecting pigeons, sparrows, starlings, crows and more. They weren't just random birds picked from trees and telephone wires, he brought only the birds mentioned in the plays of Shakespeare. That was Edward's mission, the reason for this second trip to Mars.

The elevator door slid closed behind him, he walked across the sand toward a hill. His alligator shoes slid into the loose soil.

At the top of the climb, he stopped. This was where it would start. He pictured a statue of himself placed here, and the birds that would land on him. He opened the suitcase and there were the Earth birds, dehydrated and kept in packets.

## Tips of Leaves

Two deer eating
tips of leaves
one sees me
and a spring
shoots in its leg

## A Thousand Miles from the Sea

The dark sky thundering sent everyone inside
to wait. Wooden walls shake, wheat flattens in
the strong wind, when overhead, rolled above
the hills, the whales begin appearing. Down from
the heights they play over crops like they do at sea
until one of them hits the windmill and crashes into
the ground dead. That wasn't supposed to happen
but that's the way it goes. It's over, the other whales
hide away into the black wind. Lightning swings
crazily like a lantern, clouds spread it out.
The storm passes, farm doors pop from frames,
boys and girls run outside to find the whale
washed down from the air.

## Bevo Tires

Bevo Francis could reach up through
the flowers of the magnolia tree to find a nest
in the green. When the birds were gone,
he collected their round twig homes, the trophies
of his height, to line his bedroom shelves.

Though he spent his time that way
in trees, once autumn turned the leaves brown
and brought them down, he stood out like a
ladder.

Couch Newt Oliver stepped on the brake
to stare. He even got out of the car to stand in
the cold and curling gray exhaust to make sure
it wasn't a play of daydream. He saw Bevo and
he could already read the headlines of the future.
Coach Newt spoke in awe, "This boy is going to
be a star."

People said those were his golden years,
the high school team when he played ball and
toured. He was on his way to fame, scouts from
cities were there for every Friday night game,
watching him go back and forth on the yellow
wooden floor. But Coach Newt already had Bevo
under wing. Before school even ended, they
packed bags and left with the carnival.

For years, Bevo played those fixed games
in tents for crowds of gamblers and that scene.
He rolled across the country in cars and trains
so many times until he got tired and his talent
dried. He started to miss. His legs creaked
rustily. After half an hour, he had to sit down
to hold his face in his hands. The world made
of a hundred towns began to spin.

At a Greyhound station snowy day,
a handful of rings waved a paper in front of him.

Coach Newt gave him back the contract and said,
"Where do you want to go?"
The reader board clicked destinations.
All the years had taken their toll, Bevo
didn't have to look up to know.
"Home," he said.

Bevo was there again and he owned
a tire shop off Main. His bones were just as long
but weary wearing him. Stooped as he went about,
he carried a clipboard that looked like a
playing card in his hand. But his winning game
hadn't run out. He still had it in him. If somebody
sparked his memory of the golden days, he would
take a black wheel off a stack to recall, bounce it
like a ball and shooting star it through the air.

## Hawthorn Tree

I was carrying an old wooden radio along
on a bright blue Sunday afternoon sidewalk,
looking at my shadow moving over the pale lawns.
There was a loud clack as a witch's broom hit the
middle of the street. Out of the air from nowhere.
I didn't see her though. When she fell off of it she
must have landed in a tree. Or she's holding on
desperately to the peak of a house across from me.
I thought I saw her black dress and wool sweater
as she clawed tiles, reaching over for a window,
with a foot in the rain gutter to steady herself.

## The Flowershop Quartet

For a time, I went there for flowers every day.
Being in love was connected to all those green smells
and colors. It was juicy warm inside too, the windows
steamed tropical wet, the gray city snow backed away,
turned into slush in the Spring doorway. A bell welcomes.

The four girls who work there play jazz.
It's the perfect sound for searching through all
the hemmed petals. Though daisies are all I could ever
afford, wrapped up with Thelonius Monk, tied with
white piano ribbon, from hands like these, daisies
become the very breathing air in romance.

They knew what I was there for, smiling back of course,
maybe I said so one flushed afternoon. Anyway, it was
the obvious courting of a songbird unconnected to
the peddling darkness sinking the rest of the country.
Someone in love must ride with angels. Laying in flowers
to flood with. When I stopped going, they knew.

It happened on the street when I was deep in only myself,
trying to forget. The four girls of the flowershop caught
up with me at last and reminded me not to collapse. They
had seen how I could be, it filled them to have me be that
way. Out of the black cases and old boxes, they took
gold instruments and right there shook jazz again.

## Hosanna and the Kites

As true as the stars at night, the kites flew out in the day. Hosanna was the one who spooled their hundred ropes, set them in ground and let them sink far out into the blue like colored fish high over the water that surrounded her.

What was small on the horizon, she saw churning and getting bigger and closer...

An iron pollywog chugged across the glass and stopped its eggbeater feet. A ferris wheel of water unturned, unsplashed. A puff of blue smoke in the form of a bird uncurled.

With a clang, a door on the top popped open. A man emerged and his eyes had to adjust to the light.

She could tell already that something was the matter and she didn't even have to ask. He was very lost to arrive here.

He got out and put his feet on the green land and maybe half thinking that it was a tree, put his hand around a string. It tugged. Almost a mile above, a kite shuddered its tail about with bells. It was so far away he couldn't hear it. He weaved his way through all the kite lines, he looked up and wondered if they were tied to the clouds.

Just then, he spoke, "It all went wrong and well yes, I'm running out of gas anyway...That ancient contraption won't get far."

So she walked out of the forest of birch colored kite strings and she showed him what to do. If it wasn't meant to last, then try something new that will. No time for tragic loss, just breathe and go on.

They transformed the pollywog water machine. Tied to her kites, he got back inside and moved with the wind.

## Wind Blown Poem

In his eyes he's halfway there. He has the bus pass,
boxes ready to be mailed, he told the landlord,
he was as good as gone. Still, it isn't easy to go.
He wakes at 3 AM feeling torn, staying or leaving
is a monumental choice. He couldn't fall back asleep.
At 8 AM he showed up here to talk . "When you're
old, you want to have roots," but dreams never stop
and somewhere else always has what he hasn't seen.
He told me how it began, on the farm, when an actor
appeared. Those days had circuses and traveling
sideshows and those lone heroes going from town
to town. He heard Shakespeare and Dylan Thomas,
he was swept from chaff, he was the seed to be
sown. Since then, he's done this many times,
picked up what he is and gone, turned into a
wind blown poem.

## Between the Clouds

I saw you Kerouac
at the airport
you laughed at
a little boy

I went on the plane
nobody checked my shoes
I crossed the sky
far above America

If you don't blink
you can see the way
between the clouds

## The Slow Motion Hero

He wasn't alone going slow. There were snails, shadows of clouds, the tree growing in a vacant lot, and others too who seemed to move in a dream. That was fine, but he was also more than that, if he felt the need, he could also fly.

One day a frightened woman ran up to him, "Please! You have to get help!"

His right foot left the ground, then his left. It took him two minutes to float ten feet off the ground. Though he threw himself into the motion, he was heavy. In the fur of hot air trapped over the cul-de-sac, dragonflies and bats whirred past. He droned with the paths of bumble bees, traffic of pollen, bright shafts of sunlight rushing through the chestnut leaves.

Clearing a fence over someone's back yard, a dog leaped at him until tiring of that. Gradually, he pushed his way into the crown of an apple tree overhang. His shirt got caught on a branch. A button scratched off. It would take a couple more minutes to free himself before he could continue.

Above the lawns, sidewalks and cars, over the state of hurrying America, he was the only one who could move at this incredible speed.

**Vera & Violet**

They live on a road way out in the country,
a steep roofed house under bright stars, luring
travelers. There's always someone looking for
them, after a long day, when the world's atmosphere
and gravity wears them out. Someone stops at a
telephone booth, surrounded by moths, finds their
address leafing through the book. Drive by night,
follow the evening star until you're there. A big moon
behind the bare branches of a tree, like a gigantic
dandelion ready to blow.

**A Night in Japan**

Closing the café
late at night
playing Sinatra songs
letting the candles go
while I mop the floor
and you wait for me

## Henry Fonda, 1941

Her kiss
in my dream
is all
I wanted
life to be

## The Sleepwalker's Cafe

Their doors open at night and they walk into the blue
while they're still asleep. They leave whatever life behind
when they travel under the moon to The Sleepwalker's Café.

"Pull up a chair, sweet dreamer," I say with my eyes
closed in the midst of a fantasy. We drink tea then
dance the Charleston. It's an amazing affair,
all these people are gathered here, laughing and
sighing, until the clock begins to chime and then
it's time for everyone to go back home.

In the morning, they wake up and they don't even know
their dreams were real and happen every night at
The Sleepwalker's Café.

## The Passenger Pigeon Romance

The city skyline was jagged with smokestacks and chimneys leaning off roofs. What the wind blew in was air turned out of a factory, rough and silty as sand, that settled and took hold and weighted things down. The drifting steam got into everything. Beside a little window cut in the bricks, he wrote a letter to her. By the time he finished, the page was colored with soot, some poured out the creases into the envelope. The next break in his shift, he slipped away to the tallest window and opened it. He tagged the letter to one of the company's passenger pigeons and held it towards her. The wings would whirr like an egg beater off into the gray. Anyone could see how he poured out his heart to her. He would walk into walls, stare at the sky, seem to be lost in thought. When the boss found out, he brought the bird down with a net. The old man crumpled the pigeon in his hand like paper, the note and the feathers, and shoved the death of the bird at him. It was over, he worked to finish the hours. Factory at dusk, the last embers of a worn-out sun, lamplighters working along the streets like fireflies, the coal powered dirigibles carrying workers home, clacking trains going in and out of the ground.

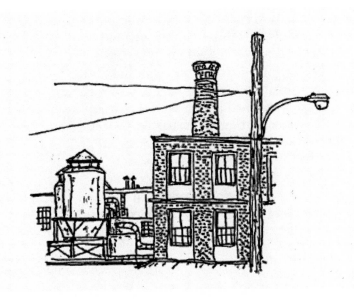

## Down by the Factory Crumbles

Down by the factory crumbles where the river
sweep washed a little higher, a little lower for
year after year, she stopped to read the rusty
tea leaves cast upon the shore. When you are
made of such as this, you think you may last
forever. Concrete will turn back into sand,
while ivy vines make veins through relics plans.
She came here everyday to play, until she grew
old enough, found love and moved away.

## A Ballet Shoe

Planted yellow flowers by the side of the road
break for a path made through the barbed wire.
There are beer bottles dashed on either side.
Hollowed, a place falls apart in trees and dirt,
the path leading straight to it. Nothing wants to
live too near a dead house, on the ground
around just dried gray leaves, broken glass
and—in the leaves—it looks like another leaf,
but when she bent down, she saw a ballet shoe.
Ancient thing, stiff and brittle with crawling
beetles. She took it though, shook it, dusted it
off to keep. Whatever had happened inside
the house, whatever life breath flew out,
leaving only fragments in the four corners,
taking away and away everything of a family,
had forgotten this ballet shoe that she put in
her pocket to bring back with her.

## Other Patches of the Sky

She lay on her back, to point at the sky.
Through the lens, all the clouds in the blue
paddled by. While she waited for the moment
to arrive. When a bird flew across the glass,
she would capture it in a photograph.
She would take it home inside the camera
and in the red lights of the dark room,
release it again to the world.
Swirled in the water and chemicals,
the bird would reemerge slowly.
Dripping, becoming real, then pinned
to dry on a singing rope with other
patches of the sky.

## Sister City

Sister City walks with the land holding skyscrapers
and shopping malls cupped in her hands. Her long
legs take her in one step into the sea. The water
climbs over her, as she flows down and her dark
hair floats around her, swimming with her hands
above the waves. She carries the city across ocean
and plants it on the shore of another continent.
The buildings left like sand castles, softened by
the clouds, she goes back underwater.


## The Duke of Earl Fable

He walks, he churns,
sainted along in slow procession
like a paddlewheel from history
in tuxedo tails, top hat and cane

With his own singing trio
to praise his name and nobility
the Duke of Earl moves on the air
over water, wherever he is needed

Peeled like a shadow from a book of royalty,
he is in the spotlight, his message is clear
and golden as the Buddha
everything is cared for
then he begins to fade away
out of this place, he can still be heard
long after the crackling end of song

## Singing Filled Leaves

I can't keep
these birds
in here

the sound
spills out
like silver
from a yellow
bucket

and singing
fills the leaves


## For a Nesting Bird

He left a dipper
in the growing fork
of a young maple tree
measuring the seasons
cupping rain or snow
until the tree grew
to the height where
the long stem handle
made a silver cradle
for a nesting bird


## Birdsongs

The radios played birdsongs, from the latest thrill
to the warbling old tunes your grandparents knew.
Even the shop on the corner would have one or two
wooden cages in eaves to speaker out music while
you buy coffee for the trip on the morning trolley.
Wintering cold with a warm cup in hand, that last
pretty song would stick in your head while you went.

## Two Grandmothers

1.
The wind wanted her birch tree
but she leaned into the hurricane
with her back against the bark
holding it safe until morning

2.
She drove that blue station wagon
with the wood paneling in slow motion
On the long stretch bordered in pine
we were passed by flocks of birds

## The Laughing Buddha

The Laughing Buddha curved with the world over
water. The steamship held a full load of mahogany
in the hull. Some of the sailors were also taking back
animals to sell in America. A monkey got loose and
lived in the network of pipes that ran vines all throughout.
Over the metal bolted doorway, a slip by the cook and
he could eat all their food tossed to him above the table.
A long voyage past mines and submarines, the oceans
turned to land. After all the unloading cranes onto train
cars, the first mate drove off with a seabag and his
Laughing Buddha set up like a wooden clock on
the dashboard. For a long time, the rest of a lifetime
flowed by like a wheel. At the end, in the last seconds,
he suddenly knew. And the Laughing Buddha sat on
the fireplace mantel next to seashells, some photos
and a gong from the Congo.

## Bob Hope's Ordinary Life

What if he never found that fame
in all the movies we know him for
if he stayed at the café, a singing waiter
until he met a pretty girl and enchanted her
he joked and only dreamed of wanting more

Reality has many possibilities
luck takes notice or stays asleep

He got another job somewhere
he witnessed all the ordinary
he has a family, he paints the house
he rakes the leaves on Saturday,
the things so many people know

Maybe he decided his life was a movie
and he played it that way, it's okay
he was never not a star, see him later
a big table, the wedding of a daughter
flowers and feast, he was asked for a speech
he was never known to pass up a microphone,
the room quieted down, the spotlight was on
Bob Hope

## Enlisted Cantaloupes

George is in his seventies and he mows our lawn
just the narrow strip of grass thatching the alley
the rest grows tall around our house and waits
for me waiting for the right time to arrive.
I finally caught up with old George
after he was done one day
and we talked under the maple tree.
He told me stories and then he took
out his wallet to illustrate one.
On the island of Tinian in 1945
a B-29 stretches silver across the runway
three engine mechanics work in the shadow.
With trembling finger George explains
that one had a wife back at home
she mailed him cantaloupe seeds in a letter.
George points at the halved out
incendiary bomb shells lining
the right side of the photograph.
You can imagine them starting to grow.
George can't remember the man's name
it was another time, so long ago
but he never forgot what happened
when all the cantaloupes were ripe.
That mechanic stood his ground
when the officers raised hell
"These are just for the enlisted," he said
and he made sure that they got them.

## George Returns

After finishing high school, he was sent to training
and flown around in a B-17. There are pictures of
him on the lawn in Peyote, Texas, hamming it up
like a movie star. After a few flights, the pilot
decided George wouldn't make it as a career
gunner. George got sick holding the machine gun
at 30,000 feet. The plane went on to England without
him. He stayed on the ground, repairing engines.
He wrote to his old B-17 friends and waited for replies.
When he received a letter, he read how the entire crew
was lost over Germany. No more has ever been known.
George was assigned to the 504th. The bombers he
worked on flew to Northern Japan and dropped
mines in the sea. The war went on. He lost planes.
There were a lot of them. They all had names and
wore paintings of women. Lost. Then all the officers
suddenly left; something so dangerous was about
to happen they moved to another island, miles
away. Mystery arrived. A single bomber landed.
It would carry one bomb to Hiroshima. Nobody
knew what would happen, either on Tinian or in
the wooden houses and streets of the Japanese
city with one day left.

## The Rain

Clouds gathered in a sky continent, anchored to the spires and sewn to air between the hills. Below, people took out umbrellas, or slid under the eaves of buildings, as they walked slouched in the wind. The first water drops stung ground and skin, then in a school of fish sweep, the rain began to melt the city. Bricks turned to oil and poured off walls. Yellow taxi cabs and grocery carts made candlewax shapes in river streets. So it's really come to this, I thought, as the vision of my everyday world blurred and stopped being a parking lot. A painting of color splashes at my feet. When the rain stopped, when the clouds unraveled into threads, the blue sky returned in moonlight. I don't know why the rain was only water to me. So many shapes washed away to become the new land, most of what used to be is gone. I could have been driven to despair to think that a world could have been formed without you, but the real miracle made it through. You survived and surprised me on a carpet of supermarket.

## Perfect Chance

Suddenly I remember that house where I worked
stuffing envelopes with a nine year old. His father,
my boss, gave me the keys to his car one time so
I could pick it up from the garage. I took the bus
there to drive his rattling, barely repaired Chevrolet
back to work. On the way, I was overwhelmed with
a vision, the temptation to run it off the floating bridge
into Lake Washington…It was my perfect chance,
a wonderful thing I've seen in movies and always
wanted to do, crash a car off into sparkling water.
Minimum wage had delivered me this possibility.
Hopefully the cement barrier would burst like
plaster. Sinking, green water flooding in through
the vents and cracked glass, I would calmly take a
deep breath, roll the window down and swim up to
the surface where news crews and stopped traffic
would be waiting for my Hollywood hero emergence…
Unfortunately, I drove back to the job, parked his car,
went inside and got handed a rake. See what I could
do with the garden, there were weeds choking the
azaleas.

## The Lucky Halibut

It sat in a lavender glow
neon and flashing window lights
the bubbles around it were frantic
the glass of its tank hummed
with strange delight

The Lucky Halibut was painted
on the sign, but nobody knew
what made it lucky or even if
it could bring luckiness to you

So there it sat, unknown in the sand
flat, held down by gallons of water
with a secret or not

## The Ugly Cat

The porch became its home day after day
and nights too. Not because it was getting
food or the best shelter in the neighborhood.
The whole thing was a mystery to Martin.
He didn't know what to do.
The ugly cat attached itself to
the wood sills of the porch like
a barnacle with crooked eyes.

## Ruby Eyes

The Tin Man is still here over in the
corner of the barn, though I don't know
if he is much remembered. After all these
years he resembles a rusted spring that
might have flowed up from caverns
underground and frozen. He's watched
his friend the Scarecrow who stayed by
dissolve gradually, he was only made of
cloth and hay. The lion had to run away
a long time ago, he didn't want to scare
anyone who might come by. Dorothy, oh
there's still the little spark held memory
of her bright in him as a lightning bug
in a jar. The barn leans more, holes let in
the sun in places, while other places get
darker shadows and one day maybe one
of those terrible storms will strike it away
with lightning into fire. But before that
possibility, one morning something else
happened. A little girl's voice carried past
the slats of wood dreamily, like a lantern
blinking in. She was singing, and she
stopped outside that corner where the
wind blew a hole in. She looked just next
to him, she got courageous enough to put
her head in. Her long brown hair, her eyes.
The Tin Man who was nearly blind, old as
sunken treasure, knew those eyes. They
shone rubies carried inside of her in a
long line of people all the way from
Dorothy.

## The Other Yard

When we lived in that other house
remembering a few years ago
our daughter learned to walk

Whenever we were outside
under the clothes flapping sails
on the windy lines off trees
she would drive herself wobbly
on to the other yard next door

The grass was all wooly around
the rickety swing set bones
standing like a dinosaur
with a slide bowing down

## Mourning Doves

They perch
on power lines
so their sorrows
are magnified
carried for miles

Far down the wire
someone will cry
and won't know why

## A Quiet Moment in 1952

The book was attached to a machine that sealed it
inside with a metal frame around so only through a
postcard shape of glass could the book be seen.
Two silver hooks swiveled inwards, touched the
cover and hovered.
Mason Hall had paid a thousand dollars for this
gray paperback from the last century. It would be
a treasure if it hadn't been opened since then.
He sought out the most unread books, appliance
agreements, manuals, or pale magazines. It wasn't
the words or thoughts but the air inside of them
that he wanted.
He patted the machine, pressed the switch
and watched the glass as the book breathed.
Immediately the machine went to work.
The infinitesimal and invisible captured on
the window became a gathering picture.
Three green walls showed, a painting of birds,
a standing lamp with a crack in the shade,
bright electric light spilled out, the corner
of a worn easy chair, the miraculous truth of
a quiet moment in 1952.

## Poe at the Zoo

It must have started on a folded scrap
with a sharpened charcoal or a nib in hand.
He made observations leaning on the metal rail
at the Paris Zoo ape house...Brute strength,
a razor and a thought chimneyed, trailing words
storied out beyond the city limits like clouds.

## Pets

Now with science we can make our own animals,
from the circus or a zoo at a size convenient for you.
Elephants are popular, shrunk down to 20 inches tall,
holding to your leg as you move from room to room
at home. A six inch whale in a goldfish bowl, spouting
every half hour like a cuckoo-clock to keep time by.
An ostrich in a canary's wooden cage, flapping its
wings in the sunlight coming through the window.
A hippo curling in your arms and purring like a cat
when its stomach is rubbed. With all the animal
kingdom to pick from, his possibilities were
exciting and pet stores took on a magical glow
like the colors and chrome of a dreamed 1956
Chevrolet showroom. He would carry home
a four inch buffalo scratching in a little paper box.
There were airholes poked in the top and as he
walked he could inspect through to see his pet
move. And he would let his buffalo loose on the gold
carpet of his bedroom floor, watching it roam
the prairie floor, past the toy model railroad
stretching from one corner to the other like
Manifest Destiny miniaturized.

## The White Plastic Horse

Here I am
with two children
quarelling over
a white plastic horse
and he wanders up

"I just rolled in
on that motor home
from Missoula
could you spare
some money
for gas?"

Here I am
with my pants
rolled up
the kids fighting
over a horse
"I'm sorry
I have nothing
right now."


Consider it a draw
a Montana cowboy
with nothing to lose
and a father like me
who begs for calm

No Western showdown
he walked off into the sun
and I'm left to lean
against the flowers

## Anyone's Poems

This evening the famous poet
reads in town ten minutes away
while I'm here in the gloom
lit only by a nightlight room
telling a bedtime story
feeling the wrong thing
wishing to hurry from here
leave my daughter awake
to go be there
even though I don't
it will take a couple days
before I finally realize
the night I stayed home
is worth more than
anyone's poems

## When Li Po Went to the Moon

He leaned over the water
to wrap his arms around

He fell in and went down
found a bone white ticket
that let him travel on

## When You Were Three

When you were three
and fell asleep
to a fable on TV

I lifted you
like a flying carpet
traveler
and carried you
easily as air

Up the stairs
thirty feet
above the street

To where
you float in dream

**Sending Hands**

Far from her
he mailed his hand
traced onto paper
then he waited
for the envelope
she would send
so he could
unwrap
hers


**A Loving Heart**

Her nightgown caught in the wave of the wind
this late at night. On the balcony, sitting there,
overlooking the rest of the town blinked in lamplight.
She stares, if that is the word, really she looks far
beyond. America isn't even a thought tonight.
As usual, her entranced life has been brought to
this place once more. There are stars. She forgets
which one is Mars. Someone told her long ago,
it's easy to find: it's as red as a loving heart.

## I Wonder Where
## You'll Be

Since I can't see you
in daylight
I search for you all night
in my sleep

...dreaming you were a talking seal
I touched your face and you said hello
soft water eyes you've seen me
...dreaming you raised wings
to fly a hundred miles per hour
I learn the touch of your hands
...dreaming we found places
with safe walls and windmills

When day arrives
the morning takes up the sky
I go to work to walk up stairs
for the cost of living I pinwheel

Then night falls
I go home and close my eyes
I wonder where you'll be

## Up and Down the Sides of Mountains

He was reckless, he walked on roofs, on the tiles
and blue shingles, next to old river gutters filled
with rain. She watched him from her window cut
into the eaves. "Stop doing that!" she said and her
windmill voice proposed, "You should be in here
instead." Opening the rainbow colors of her
curtains, he saw her leaned heavenly in the sun.
That was it, he was falling. He took the steep last
walk past the scarecrow of television antennas
to where she smiled, flowerboxed out over
the window ledge.

## The Music of Her Clock

He needed to open the window a bit it was so hot. She could only sleep in tropical heat, all night long the iron grill at the foot of their bed would blow. At five o'clock the music of her clock would wake her and slowly she would roll away from him to the shower, while he slept on. Irene had left for work already, by now she was at the café serving early breakfast.

Ray peeled off the sheet and stuck his legs out onto the black carpet. The only light in the room came from the red digital clock glow. The dark windows rattled a storm blowing up off the lake. Out there, waves would be crashing all over the shore. Ray pulled up the window, cold air rushed inside. The rose tree scratched against the glass.

He crawled back under the covers, lying over the warm shape left on her side of the bed. He fell asleep again.

A window shutter banging woke him up.

The room, a shade of blue, was very cold. A few leaves had blown inside. Silhouettes of furniture, the purple dresser and the bookshelf against the wall. At least an hour must have passed since he opened the window. He had a thought of Irene serving eggs to people as he dragged himself to the window and shut it.

When he was back in bed he heard the purr from the corner. A cat had curled herself there on the tangle of clothes. She must have come in out of the storm, Ray wondered, rolled over, and went back to sleep.

Colors and visions turned in his dream and became a tall metal bridge he was walking on. Underneath, riverwater rolled, carrying houses, cars, parking lots, stores, an entire slow town drifting past. Then his alarm clock bell went off and he reached out of the dream to hit it off.

Irene had her clock to go to work by and Ray had his. Ray yawned, stretched away. The room was warm again at eight o'clock. Already he had forgotten his dream, but there opposite him was the cat. Sometime since her arrival through the cold window, he could hear the small noises, there was now a kitten. Ray came closer to her and saw the one white pearl against her side.

## The Opening Act

In Ohio, the famous State Theater glows beside
Lake Erie. It has been open from Vaudeville and
the Depression to this very end of the 20$^{th}$ Century.
A crowd of bright colors bent to the ticket windows
to pay twenty dollars each and go inside. What
brought us there too was the mothlike appearance
of the Smothers Brothers. Jostling among the senior
citizens for a while, we hoped for a white haired
scalper or tickets to fall somehow on marble floor.
When we were alone, everyone was deep inside
the theater watching the red curtains and gold
carvings, we decided to sneak in. Around the
corner, we found a gray service door propped
open with a little block of wood. I opened it
scarcely and saw red uniforms dressed like
decoys weighted down in chairs in the hallway.
Also, a man with thick black glasses had spotted
me and was bearing down like one of Roosevelt's
dreadnoughts.
I hopped backwards and scooped my wife's hand.
We hurried down the length of theater and around
into the parking lot. I looked back over my shoulder
and saw the door just beginning to open, slowly.
We were safe. A dangerous looking fire escape
clung to all the bricks running towards the roof.
We could hear applause washing inside the theater.
Past the next corner at the side of the wall, we
discovered a stage door there. We were so close
we listened to the heavily bolted metal and heard
the familiar guitar and bass and voices from records.
I put my hand on the door and for a few seconds
considered what would happen if I opened it.

## While the World Was
## Busy Being Painted

There are a few moments
just before dawn when
a furious construction
job goes on

The world is mended
and painted and readied
for the day

She found out
by accident
walking to school

A paintbrush
left by the road

She picked it up
the secret revealed
it was wet with fruit

She could paint blackberries
on anything it touched
until the paint dried out

## The Mermaid Relocation Program

Someone discovered her in the reservoir,
sometimes it happened in a swimming pool,
there was a lake they liked to show up in too.
A red truck drove there, they caught her and
put her in a tank in the back. It was still early
in the morning, whoever else was around
didn't pay much attention, the morning was
gray and cold. They drove to the ocean and
lifted her down. All that water poured out,
she went with it, in the flood from the bin.
It happened so often they could make their
living from it.

## Saint of the Roses

Scraping paint on the barn
jammed against the lilacs
and the red flower thorns
on the top ladder rung
the whole thing slipped
and suddenly I had
a vision old as holiness
the Saint of the Roses
appeared in that second
to stay the silver legs
and stop my fall

## At Last the Year 1923

Andrew always wore a cardigan and like a mother
kept Jocko safe in there. Going up country his pet
caused a stir riding in the open touring car.
Arriving in New Hampshire, swimming in the river
to cool off the hot air, Jane's white legs were nipped
underwater. At last the year 1923, when Andrew died,
his dearest friend cried and cried. A broken heart,
alone, so sad without him. It must seem like a dream
to know about these things happening. Once upon an
afternoon the family would gather together at the zoo
to go see Jocko and so remember Andrew.

## October Leaves

There are still
some robins
left in the tree

They hold on to
the bare branches
like orange brown leaves
the October wind
will blow away

## The Cardboard Violin

Myrtle Beet was done making a cardboard violin. Nobody was there to ask her about it, the long hours it took to construct and paint and string. While it rested like an elegant duck on her counter top, she could admire it and breathe all the satisfaction she needed. What a marvelous and perfect imitation, she had even detailed the wood grain, she knew anybody looking at it would never know. She smiled then at that. Yes, there was one who would know. Soon enough.

She reached and pulled the heavy black telephone across closer to her. A trembling finger found the numbers and dialed them. It hadn't been easy keeping arthritis and old age at bay while she built the violin.

"Hello," she said when the ring turned into him. "Hello Leonard, it's Myrtle Beet. How are you dear?" In the pause, the clock in the kitchen wall tocked. "Well," she said, "Why don't you come over here. I have a present for you." She smiled. "Yes, alright. See you soon." She hung up and watched the violin, pleased with herself.

In a minute, the apartment door started to scratch into a couple of knocks.

Myrtle stood up slow, straightened her dress and the apron she wore. She glanced at the violin again, she could almost hear it already.

She put her hand around the glass diamond door knob and turned.

The man who spent all of his time in the apartment next door stood there. He was frail and gray from lack of sun and wind and rain, he was Leonard the cardboard man.

## The Bicycle Tomb

We came home to find a man with a broken foot
clawing through the boxes in our backyard shed.
It wasn't something I wanted to see, or the yellow
lopsided truck in the alley. He muttered the word
for bicycle, he forgot it in there when he used to
rent this house. Behind the wall of dead cardboard,
the Edgar Allan Poe of bicycles was a frightening sight.
All rust and broken ribs and bends and tangled over
with black veins of dead berry thorns. He clubbed
his tragic mummy foot over the stones unsteadily
with the bicycle in his arms. I put it in the truck bed
for him. It wasn't much, it must have meant more
in memories.

## Sam the Canary

The song seemed to have flown out of
Sam the canary. He stared out the cage
past the tapestry that mapped the wall.
A memory. A place far away and over
a sea of threads and patterns. It would
take all the wind in his wings to get him
there again.

## Hunting Bat

Last night I happened downtown to hear
Richard Mallory read his poetry. He would be later,
so I waited outside on the dark street corner.
That's how I was staring at the Federal Building
and I discovered they have a vampire in there.
Believe me, there was no mistaking the uniform,
he looked like a Bela Lugosi movie. How could I be
the only one around watching this? I saw him creep
across the window. I couldn't tell if he was leaving,
he got lost in the murky green light and shadows.
I wondered what he did, I guess that was obvious,
I took a look at the sky for the blackbird shape of
a hunting bat. I got a little nervous, I heard something,
I turned around and hurried back into the café.

## Mr. Fritz's Bug

Observing the flights that raced across his retina,
Mr. Fritz finally eased out of his hammock. He had
nothing else to do this lazy day. First he put a thick
lens invention in front of his eye. The world jumped
with details. He fine tuned the box all the wires ran to.
The connection created vision made of horizontal
lines that he could follow like yarn in a maze left
behind. Taking up the fading thread of one, he
pursued it across the field, along the dazzling wall
of garden flowers to where it landed on mossy bark
of an old elm tree. He tuned the dials to see more
clearly what was happening on the trunk. The line
ended in a little green bug who had flown all the way
here. It waved its six legs to another bug it met and
Mr. Fritz had to zoom in close for this astonishment.
The bug whose life he had chose to chase, pulled out
a blur of something and had it punched in the smallest
machine. It passed the timecard to another bug,
who then counted out frail scales of money. Mr. Fritz's
bug stuffed them under its wing and sprang with a joy
off back into the wind.

## Old Time

Crows perched
on telephone poles
guarding subterranean
cathedrals lurked
beneath blackberry

The ground
transmitting
kept vibrant
while we run
overhead in cars

There are
beauties concealed
by vines and thorns
old time fairy tales
are real

## Sleep and the Monsters

The floor in front of the glow
watching the late night show
for us the vow of staying awake
while sleep and the monsters
meet on the screen
and turn into a dream

## Rocketman Remembered

How he used to leap
and we tried to repeat
that jump on concrete

## How Come?

I wasn't on television for very long
I was on a local program called *How Come?*
making a giant pair of inflatable sunglasses.
A few seconds worth of film for the day,
they may have been hoping for more,
a shot of the boy levitating dramatically
riding the sunglasses out of the room
and into the air for a slow dissolving
pan of him disappearing into sky.

## Linda Johnson

I took advantage of Linda Johnson

Each morning I would wave goodbye
at my parents house and walk a block
to Linda's house. She had a color TV
a warm breakfast and a ride to school

That's all she meant to me and
after third grade she was forgotten

## The Bee Ring

Once when I was climbing
a hill I sunk my hand
into the leaves and out
I withdrew a bumblebee
sitting royally on my finger

Afterwards
I wore the sting
the numb fire there
like a ring


## The Salmon

The salmon is still
the dream fish
swimming into
the sleep of even
a three year old
who tells the story
when he wakes
in the morning


## Lunch Break

He sits on a white
plastic bucket
with a knife

If anybody
needs him up
on the scaffold
they have to wait
for the apple
to be peeled
and eaten

## The Tallest Shoes

He had shoes that made him the second tallest person in the state. The tallest person in the state was a woman down the coast about an hour away. He tried not to think about her achievement, it grieved him. It wasn't as pleasurable as it used to be to step over high tension wires, walk over gas stations and startle people in their apartments at night. What used to be the source of such great pride, to stride with those towering feet, just didn't feel as impressive anymore. Someone was taller, someone else could see further.

Finally, he couldn't stand it anymore. It was dangerous, it meant a whole new realignment of balance (with pulleys and propellers and swinging pendulum weights) but he did it: he added twelve more feet to his shoes. "Now..." he issued a challenge through the window of the newspaper skyscraper, "What does she think of this?!"

But it was all over the news the next day, she was walking twenty feet taller than him, feeding pigeons from the clouds. And she was graceful with her height, like a Japanese crane, a thing of beauty moving. All the more furious it made him, to watch her glide so effortlessly across the silver television screen. He added another thirty feet to his shoes, stood, swayed and fell backwards, crashing down through a greenhouse.

Still plucking cactus spines from his skin, he worked late into the night until a fantastic blueprint emerged. On paper, he would be fifty feet taller than her. All the stainless steel, fiberglass, rockets, electronics and robotics would make him the tallest person in the state by far. When he finished building the shoes, he folded them into a box that he squeezed into the trailer of a rented semi-truck. "Never has there been a bigger pair of shoes!" he shouted into his C.B radio. People passing by in their cars waved at the truck painted *God Bless Our Tall Shoes!* Off the highway, down the mainstreet of her town, he rolled the truck right onto her front lawn and marched up to her door.

When she opened the door, he didn't know what to say. She had never appeared to him like this before, smiling, curving in her flowered doorway. "Come in," she radiated, "I've been expecting you, knowing you'd show up sooner or later." She led him to a chair and he sat down.

"I've never seen you from the ground," he said to her. He thought in amazement, "All of a sudden, I feel very differently about you."

She was sitting just across from him and looking at him too. She asked, "You're probably angry that my shoes are taller, aren't you?"

There were pictures on the walls, designs and creations he could never have imagined. Her house was filled with so many ideas. "I don't mind..." he smiled at her, though something almost made him cry out loud, "But I have a pair of shoes in the truck that are the tallest!" No, he didn't want any more competition. He would find some deep water and lay those tall shoes of his quietly to rest. Then they wouldn't talk about shoes anymore.

## Outnumbered

All he had to do was open the door to her
store wearing a number 15 on his striped
shirt. She eyed him mercurially, and asked
him about it. He admitted he got the little
numbers at a sewing shop, that's all, and
they talked and had coffee and listened to
Sinatra on the radio. She kept him going
in coffee and poured cups for other friends
who stopped by.
When he opened the door the next day
she was wearing a red shirt with a 16
stitched to it.
"Hey!" he said.
She brought their coffees and sat down
with him.
The day after, he came by and sat
in the same kitchen chair.
It was her turn to be surprised.
He had sewn a zero to the end of 15
to make it 150.
She seemed slow preparing their coffee.
He looked at shoes. She acted busy.
The next day was rainy. He was thinking
he better get a job soon, for rent and food
and the other things that came with a price.
He was looking forward to the bicycle ride
in the rain though. He even put on his striped
number 150 shirt again.
He rode in under the eaves and parked and
left the bike leaning against a cold mannequin.
The door chimed him in. The store was a lot
warmer than the fall out there and he could
smell coffee brewing.
Behind the counter, she called hello to him.
She had a string of a billion numbers running
across her chest like a necklace.

## Kentucky Street All Stars

How would I describe this street? No surprise.
Telephone poles, a couple cars parked along
the curb. Fencing, metal buildings, storage,
equipment rental, a plumbing office with a
red and white truck. At the end of the street,
a few square houses, fir trees, all the colors
are browns and grays. Topped on the black
distant hill, snow in the clearcut, clouds in
a dull sky.

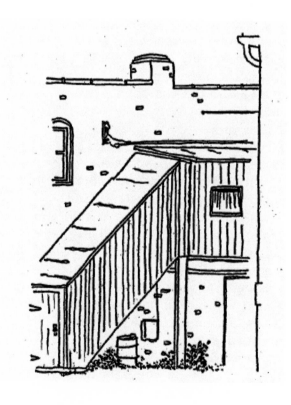

## The History of Motown

For too long, I lived in a basement apartment in a
tenement house. $175 a month for roaming spiders,
a bed made out of a shot-down biplane, a kitchen
seeped in layers of fish oil, etc. etc. But I can't be
too cruel about it, because there I was, for too long,
my mind stuck in the overwhelming grief of my friend
who had died and feeling like I was dead too, in that
tomb. But I did write while I was there: *The Sand Rivers*,
*Salmon of the Future*, *Believing in Windows*, the *COW*
magazines and all the books: *The Creation of the World*,
*Poems in Zoos*, *Lawn Veterans*, *The Shrinkers*, *Waterhouse*,
*Paying For Water*, *The Last Frankenstein*, *The Time Has
Come To Make All The Machines Fly*, *Tree Frog* and more
poems and things. Still, it was hellish. I had this idea
that some beautiful vision would materialize and
drag me out of there. I was very wrong about that.
It was a bad time, the only way out was to help myself...
I was working washing dishes when a friend told me
about a house in Ballard. Quickly, I went back to my
underground room, dragged out my things and a
mattress, stuffed everything into a VW and got caught
by my landlord. We didn't leave on the best of terms,
she looked like a furious Grand Old Opry. But I was
free at last! The same old song began...Only two of us
paid rent, we couldn't afford heat, it was dead winter.
America invaded Kuwait and bombed Iraq. A huge
snowstorm hit Seattle and buried us. We burned our
couch and kept the oven open, always on, for warmth.
There was an artificial leg hanging in the window.
I wrote three books. *Good Deed Rain*, *Fish Bicycle*, and
*Water Everywhere*...Then 'Waldo' went on the rampage,
he told us he could channel plants and he took a bottle
of wine and left to court the lead singer of Heart,
tracking her down to her mansion, lurking outside
her gates like a shadow. It was bad...I found out about
another house, immediately I moved in. A blue
carpeted bedroom, heat pouring out of a metal vent,
blinking Christmas lights twined around Buddha statues.
Food Giant was just two blocks away. I played records

in the morning, drinking tea, petting the cat named Pearl.
For a while it seemed almost calm. The Spring arrived
and I wrote the *Flora Rabinovitch* book and poems
like *The Doghouse* read under the monorail at night.

## Miles To Go Before We Sleep

I found out all I ever knew about her in the short span
of a week. In the cold winter, I had moved into what
used to be her room. The relief of getting into a space
of my own was so incredible, I concentrated just on
the miraculous working of the heat vent and all the blue,
soft carpeted floor space. Finally, I could rest. I didn't
concern myself with who lived there before me.
Though she left a few things in the closet which I
discovered: a black and white xerox of an Aztec
dancing skeleton and a jacket which fit me. One day
I wore it to the bus stop and I stuck my hand in the
pocket. A clear plastic hospital bracelet with her name
on it. Then someone told me about her. She had just
been released from the institution, also, barely twenty,
she already had two babies and she was pregnant again
(she didn't seem to care, she gave them up for adoption).
And now, she was returning to the house for a week,
before joining her parents down in Costa Rica.
I wondered if she would want to stay in her old room,
maybe I should give it back to her. I didn't want to
upset her, I try to be kind to people who have swirled
under. Monday, I dragged home from work, my hands
stinging from chlorine and the cold and I opened the
door and there she awaited. Her shaved head was
glued closely to the TV screen, watching Jeopardy.
It didn't seem necessary for her to know we were
there in the room with her, but I said hello. For a long
time before she arrived, I'd been thinking about that
shadowland pulling at us like a whirlpool, how careful
you need to be, but she had plunged herself into its river,
the entire week all she did was watch the television,
whatever was on. I would go to sleep and I could hear
her bedded down in front of the glow, laughing on
and on at *Ed McMahon's Star Search*.

**Directed by Stanley Lagoon**

There was a time
when men lit cigarettes
in shadows on wharves
women reflected the moon
audiences watched beneath
a glowing avenue of black & white

Everything was different
it seems only yesterday
but it was another age

Rivers are ever moving
they change direction
we are only
in the way

## The Owl

A stir in the woods
a bark colored owl
on the limb above me

We lock eyes
the face of the forest
we speak this way

There's a prayer
for these things
that's understood
everyone should know

Then I say
I have to go
I take a step
and watch
the owl fly

I am amazed
there's no sound
as he leaves
from me to
a branch
over there

## 7 A.M.

The rain starts
rattles the holly

crosses the street
to fall on me

## Rent Again

I don't know
the story behind it
I can't say why
they had to go

Their house is for rent again
tracks crushed across the lawn
where things were pulled to a truck
a plastic swimming pool is left
beside the telephone pole
filled with children's toys
a cardboard sign
says **Free**

## Uncle Charley

I wonder what
he thought about
early morning
walking around
the big metal
bomber planes
before they flew

When did
something
dawn on him
wake him up
and shine
on wings
like bolted
English dew

## The Blue Egg

Life is
going on
as sure
as dying

Always
keep trying

Knowing
the effort
of Earth
is in the smallest
crackline faults
that breathe
across us

## The Perfect Language

A 3-year-old
talking and singing

A 10-year-old
dreaming out loud

## Warm

Be excited
to speak
good things
if you can
imagine
your words
held cupped
around
a tinder
in the rain
and when
you talk
your breath
keeps it warm

## Quasimodo's Clams, Cakes & Coffee

Across the ocean spread from France, he swung in the radar belfry of the choppy steamship. With the wide Atlantic green and blue around him, lashing wind in his ragged velvet clothes, Quasimodo laughed at the wild thoughts of America. When the boat arrived in New York, all the immigrants stared in wonder at the new world that had formed out of the sea. They all fell into lines with their bags, passports and papers to hurry their way off the ramp.

But where was Quasimodo? Down in that crowd, slowly unwinding, tugging at each other and talking in excited languages? No, he was already on his way. Even in this foreign confusion, he found the shadows were still his friends and when he moved from the ship, he was helped along so nobody saw him dash over the water, crabwalk lurchingly through boxes unloading and crowds amazed by tall buildings.

He hopped onto the bumper of a passing Greyhound bus. Up the chrome rungs, he clambered to the roof and flattened out for the ride. For days, the coach kept going west. It showed Quasimodo his big and strange new land, windswept for thousands of miles all the way to where the ground sank into sea. This was it. Twilight formed a perfect postcard dream of that American beauty that's seen in movies. Quasimodo fit right in, he set up a little boardwalk stand, he hung the golden frame of success around himself. And every day a smiling, pretty Esmeralda strolled across the sand in her white sundress to share coffee and cakes along the Pacific beach.

## Humanous Lives

We became amateur Doctor Frankensteins one hungry
night, playing Gods, creating new life. What we had
wanted to begin with was simply a soup that could last
all week. "It's okay, so it's more of a stew than a soup."
That wooden spoon was getting stuck as I tried to stir it.
And he kept adding more rice, "I think it needs more
curry." Something primeval was bubbling in the pot
and finally we gave up and banished it to the frozen
wastelands of the fridge...There was still no food in
the cupboards though and in desperation it wasn't
long before we took a daring new look at the soup/stew.
As it glowed and growed on the refrigerator shelf in
a thick, silver spacesuit helmet-like cooking bowl,
I said it was luminous.
"What?"
"I said it's luminous in there."
He laughed. "I thought you said it's humanous."
It shifted uneasily towards its name, making a sloshing sound.
Fortunately, no vengeful mob of angry townspeople
with torches was necessary to kill Humanous. No terrifying
chase across rocks to a burning windmill. Humanous was
buried in the garbage bag and dumped like a pirate's
fool's gold on the sidewalk at midnight.
No mad scientist can again release Humanous on the world,
there is no recorded recipe. There will be no:
*Son Of Humanous*
No:
*The Curse Of Humanous*
No:
*I Was A Teenage Humanous*
And no:
*Humanous vs. Rodan*
Humanous will not return like black and white 1950s sci-fis.
It will not arise from the ocean or out of a landfill. It will be
discovered by archaeologists in 3012 A.D and wrongly
identified as Post-Modern Art.

## Echo of the Humanous

Humanous, the luminous human, so bright and fiery
he turns his friends into their shadows on the floor,
makes anything into instant candle wax. Before him,
a thick oak door will melt into brown, and as he passes
through, the room will become a sea of colors of what
once was there. Poor Humanous hasn't talked to anyone
in burned away calendar months...Not since he stood
at the edge of that waterfall canyon (glowing from his
heat like a lighthouse in a pack of crayons) and shouted
across to somebody who would answer him seconds later.
But it may have been just an echo.

## All America

Seen in a leaf
colors, tatters
blown by the wind

This one
fallen
on the ground
I step around

Look up
there's another
budding
on the limb

## Fired

George the cook used to burn the big pots and
there was no amount of scrubbing I could do
to clean them. Every shift I would have to leave
them sitting, soaking with soap in the sink.
The next shift began when high school let out
and the girl, I think her name was Maria,
would let me have it with the dark of her eyes.
George was a good egg, he felt bad when
I got the speech from the boss. I patted him
on the shoulder when I had to go.

## Sorting

Once in a while one of the twins would appear.
After a few mistakes, I began to tell them apart.
The store manager had a more tired look in his eyes.
His brother would show up sometimes in a blue car
to take a girl upstairs where there was a fan and
a big unmade bed. It was summer so he would
show up a lot. The twins would joke and stand
side by side and there would be the usual
easy going confusion they were so used to.
Then everyone would go back to work.
Depending on the time, I would either stock
shelves or the cooler, or sit at the register
with Barb who liked to read a paperback.
If not that, I'd be in the back to sort returns.
There was a row of barrels in the narrow
loading bay and bottles and cans had to be
sorted and tossed in by manufacturer.
I kept the door open to outside. Out there
it was green and blue and yellow and if
I was lucky there would be a breeze.
Otherwise, it was hot and the sour smell
would surround. Every few days a man
and his partner would appear. A little man
with a thick Maine accent and weathered
clothes who did all the talking. Beside him,
taller and never speaking, the man he called,
"his Indian." Of course I read books and I knew
*Of Mice and Men* and there was a real history
for these two. Almost everything has been
recorded before. The little man took his partner
along the roads searching the shoulders and
the ditch weeds not more than throwing distance
from cars. Any sign of glittering aluminum or
glass meant 5 cents. Sometimes I would see them
when I rode my bicycle home, sometimes they
would be miles from the store, dots in a field.
Showing up with plastic bags, I would calculate
through the sticky clanking piles and then
back to the register I would pay them off.

It was always the little guy who held out his hand.
I don't know if his partner got a reward, I don't
know their story, whatever kept them together
counted on a handful of paper dollars and coins.


## Captain Ben

Captain Ben didn't like to call attention
but it was a fact, he never sat on a chair.
Any summer day he came visiting, he would sit
on the porch with everyone. They'd play cards
with him down on the floor. I used to listen to them
talk and laugh out there. When it was my grandfather's
orange-lit cigarette and dark green window shadows,
Ben would stand to go home, out through the yellow
light of the kitchen, into nighttime. Did he drive back
standing up, in a convertible leaning into the wind?
No. He walked up the broken seashells on the path
to the road. He didn't need wheels to get home,
he just crossed the street, no chairs in the way.


## Captain Ben's House

Sometimes we'd go to Ben's house at dusk,
a brown galleon perched on the vertical cliff,
with a book full of pirates in a room upstairs.
The strangest thing over there was outside,
built in the yard was a big dollhouse likeness.
It seemed less of a wonder than a haunted house,
eerie little lights could click on in the rooms,
making miniature shadows out of real places inside.
We looked for ourselves, trapped on those stairs
or hallways. Mosquitoes came out of the pines
to feed on us. It was always a relief when
summer ended the sight of it, when
a big wooden box was placed over it,
to hide it from the elements.

## Island off Maine

We sailed over to
an island off Maine
a little cove set in
rocks and sumac
growing wild

I caught the bow
when we rode
onto sand

Bumped
into memory

My father
and his best friend
knew this island
long before me


## Benign Time Travel

They turn you into a sort of a ghost so there's
really nothing more you can do. Observe the world.
Float unseen except to a few. To them you may be
no more than a faint glassy shine moved along
the wall. In those moments you travel, you will
experience wonder. You may want to go back
again and again. They never seem to let you stay
long enough. Of course their machines will return
you for air in the place where you're from. Then
sign on the line, you will pay as you go, follow
what you are missing, fade into your favorite world.

## What Did I Do There?

I kept the door open
all night I listened
to the waves and
the croaking song
in the morning
the doves and
mynah birds
woke me up
then I went
for a swim

## The Dalai Lama Visit

Living in Seattle then
I was walking downtown
under the monorail

A burst of yellow light
the thin trees captured
in concrete all rattled
leaves were following
the wake of his car

## The Movie Mike Made

There should be a place
one in every town
where the heartbroken
wonders go

It should be a garden
but instead of flowers
there will be words
next to things like
the movie Mike made

Formed miraculously
when he was twenty one
stop animation with music
you couldn't keep track
if you tried on a watch
all the hours he poured
into wanting her to see

He gave her the movie
and she lost it
carelessly

In this park
love remains
memorials kept
in treasured rows
holy light of the young
like lanterns all aglow

Author photo by Rosa Luna Frost

**Allen Frost** lives in Bellingham, Washington, with wife Laura, daughter Rosa and son Rustle. He was born in La Jolla, California, and graduated from Bowdoin College in Maine. He has lived and worked in Seattle, Washington; Portland, Oregon; and Huron, Ohio. He works in the library at Western Washington University. His *Ohio Trio: Fictions* appeared in 2001 from Bottom Dog Press, followed by *Bowl of Water* written between 1989-2002. *Another Life* is drawn from limited edition poetry chapbooks written 2002-2007. Allen collects old recordings.

**Bird Dog Publishing**

*Faces and Voices: Tales* by Larry Smith
1-933964-04-9   136 pgs. $14

*Second Story Woman: A Memoir of Second Chances*
by Carole Calladine
978-1-933964-12-6   226 pgs. $15

*256 Zones of Gray: Poems*
by Rob Smith
978-1-933964-16-4   80 pgs.  $14

*Another Life: Collected Poems* by Allen Frost
978-1-933964-10-2   176 pgs. $14

*Winter Apples: Poems* by Paul S. Piper
978-1-933964-08-9   88 pgs.  $14

*Lake Effect: Poems* by Laura Treacy Bentley
1-933964-05-7   108 pgs. $14

*Depression Days on an Appalachian Farm: Poems*
by Robert L. Tener
1-933964-03-0  80 pgs. $14

*120 Charles Street, The Village:*
*Journals & Other Writings 1949-1950* by Holly Beye
0-933087-99-3   240 pgs. $15

**Bird Dog Publishing**
A division of Bottom Dog Press, Inc.
PO Box 425/ Huron, Ohio 44839
Order Online at:
**http://smithdocs.net/BirdDogy/BirdDogPage.html**

Printed in the United States
135133LV00003B/26/P